Cold Jac

To
Gwen and Bleddyn Lewis

First Impression – 2002
Second Impression – 2004

ISBN 1 84323 117 4

This title was first published with the support of the
Arts Council of Wales.

Cover design: Olwen Fowler

Printed in Wales at
Gomer Press, Llandysul, Ceredigion

Cold Jac

Rob Lewis

PONT

Jac lived on a farm on a hilltop in Wales
where chilly winds blew, and often gales.
The animals huddled and shivered and froze,
while Jac had a permanent drip on his nose.

His Nain phoned one night, saying, 'How are you, lad?
I can hear your teeth chattering. Things must be bad.'
Said Jac, 'Nights are cold, Nain.
And days aren't much better.'
'Don't worry,' said Nain, 'I'll knit you a sweater.'

Now Nain hadn't knitted for quite a long while.
She rummaged through drawers and found an old file.
The patterns she had were for socks and a vest.
'Oh well,' said Nain bravely, 'I'll just do my best.'

A parcel arrived in the very next post.
Jac read Nain's letter while eating his toast.
'Oh dear,' wrote Nain, 'I got carried away.
I made two extra armholes, I'm sorry to say.'
Jac tried it on and said, 'Wow! Look at that!
It's perfect for warming the cold tabby . . .

CAT!'

Jac telephoned Nain and said, 'Two armholes, please.'
'No problem,' she said. 'I can do that with ease.'
She knitted the sweater all day and all night
but she sewed up the armholes and made them too tight.
'Oh no!' cried Jac. 'Nain's done it again!
But at least it's the right size for Heulwen the . . .

HEN!'

'Fine, Jac,' said Nain when he gave her a call.
'I'll use bigger needles. Then it won't be so small.'
Nain worked for hours. She wouldn't give in,
but she knitted a sweater too airy and thin.
Jac opened the parcel quite early next day.
He held up the sweater and said with dismay,
'A sweater with holes I don't think I'll keep . . .'
But it stopped the wind blowing the wool off his . . .

SHEEP!

Using small needles Nain stitched more and more
'til the knitting she'd knitted reached down to the floor.
'Sorry,' wrote Nain, 'I think something went wrong.
Now the chest is too wide and the arms are too long.'
'It's too big,' said Jac. 'But I'll use it somehow.
The fit will be perfect for Ceridwen the . . .

COW!'

With practice Nain's skill had improved bit by bit.
The next sweater that came was a fantastic fit.
Jac was delighted. He wore it in bed.

He wore it outside when the animals were fed.

It stayed on all month 'til it needed a clean.
Then he washed it on HOT in the washing machine.
But when it came out he wailed round the house,
'Now all it fits is the little brown . . .

MOUSE!'

'Wash it on WARM,' said Nain. 'You'll discover
your sweater won't shrink – now I'll knit you another.'
But Nain soon found out she could not knit a thing,
because all she could find was a small piece of string.
'Jac,' said Nain sadly, 'my cupboard was full,
but now I'm afraid I have run out of wool.'
'Don't worry,' said Jac. 'I'm as cosy as can be . . .

All of the animals moved in with me!'